Best wishes to
Tony Enjoy
John [illegible]
3/3/2011

KNIGHT OF THE DRAGON RED

Story of Knights

John Tuskin

authorHOUSE®

AuthorHouse™ UK Ltd.
500 Avebury Boulevard
Central Milton Keynes, MK9 2BE
www.authorhouse.co.uk
Phone: 08001974150

First published by AuthorHouse 1/25/2011.

ISBN: 978-1-4567-7260-4 (sc)
ISBN: 978-1-4567-7261-1 (dj)
ISBN: 978-1-4567-7262-8 (e)

Chapter One

In a land of brave men who are of good and evil there lived a servant boy, who of no fault of his own was orphaned at an early age. Being average for his height and with very strong facial features and with a body other men would yearn for, his name was Ixor. Now, at the age of twelve, he was being forced to work for an evil woodman in and around the forests in the land of Rayen.

One day whilst chopping fallen tree logs on the far outskirts of the forest, he was approached by a group of three men on horseback, dressed in suits of armour. These men were knights all armed with swords, shields and lances. Upon each shield was a crest to represent the knight's title. They looked very impressive almost imposing. Fearing for his life Ixor started to run back through the forest until he reached the woodman's cottage where he took refuge inside. Upon entering he startled the woodman who was tucking into some food on the table, suddenly the door flew open and one of the knights barged in holding his sword in one hand and a bag of what looked like money in the other hand, he then threw the bag upon the table in front of the woodman and remarked "We have come for the boy." Without moving the woodman replied." Take him he's yours to do as you want with." Ixor became confused and froze where he stood at the same time the knight bound Ixor's hands with twine then led him through the door to the outside where the other knights were waiting. Startled and shocked Ixor still found it in himself to ask." What do you want, where are you taking me?" The knight who was holding Ixor's entwined hands remarked, "Keep quiet, your questions will be answered when we reach our destination." With that he pulled Ixor to his horse and tied Ixor with a long cord to the horse's girth just under the saddle, then said, "This is to stop you running away." He then climbed onto his horse. The other two knights said nothing, which made Ixor uneasy. Their silence was just as frightening as their appearance. Ixor then found himself being towed at a casual pace behind the horses back through the forest and beyond.

In all Ixor's life he had never ventured beyond the forest, he never needed to even though his master the woodman treated him bad he still had food and security. This experience had confused him so much he was still not thinking straight and these knights on horses were not going to give him any answers, of that he was sure.

After travelling for some distance, which seemed a lifetime to Ixor, he could see on the horizon some very large hills towards which the knights and he were heading. All of a sudden one of the knights' horses twisted its leg on a small boulder and became lame making it impossible to carry on, this knight was Sir Blades, displayed on his shield was an oak tree, and from his helmet flowed green plumage.

Ixor did not know it then but this knight was the green knight and one day would see him again but not for the time being because they had to leave him behind to find his own way back.

When the two remaining knights and Ixor reached the hills, both knights dismounted from their horses and began to walk up a rough path through the hill with Ixor and their horses, on reaching the top they could see in the distance a large castle in the middle of a clearing surrounded by a forest. Ixor had never seen anything like it before and became more curious than frightened, he asked again to the knight, "Are we going there?" The knight replied, "Yes, we are, but all your questions will be answered when we get there."

On reaching the castle the two knights and Ixor waited for the drawbridge to be lowered, they then entered where they were met by two squire's who took the knights horses to the stables somewhere at the side of the castle court yard. At the same time one of the knights placed their shields and lances into the armoury. Ixor had noticed the crest on each shield one had the sun burst represented as the yellow knight because that knight had a yellow plume in his helmet, the other shield had a clump of bluebells to go with the blue plume in his helmet making him the blue knight. As they walked through the courtyard amongst the daily work of servants, squires and castle guards, the knights led Ixor to a flight of steps at the main building facing them in the middle of the yard. When reaching the top of the stairs a door opened, there facing them was an elderly man dressed in the finest of clothes. "Take the boy to the main hall the king wants to see him right away." said the man.

Walking through corridors the blue knight who was Sir Bellingham and the yellow knight who was Sir Raymond still in full armour with Ixor still bound the three of them reached the main hall, before they entered both knights removed their helmets then knocked on the door in front of them.

"Enter." Was the reply from a very deep voice. On entering directly in front of them over by the far wall at a very large long table sat the king an elderly man dressed in the finest of clothes. He had long greying hair that covered his shoulders, his nose was long which made his eyes sink further into his face. Both knights bowed and then the knight who still had Ixor bound by the hands said. "Sire this is the boy you sent us to get we also had to leave Sir Blades behind, his horse became lame." The king looked sternly at them and replying said. "Who told you to tie the boy up, release him at once then go until I call for you," Realizing their mistake the two knights left, but not until they had untied Ixor.

"Please sit down. Would you like some food and something to drink?" asked the king Ixor was hungry and had no hesitation in saying yes. The king shouted towards a door at the rear of the hall and a servant appeared carrying a tray loaded with food and water. "Help yourself." said the king, just as the servant placed the tray on the table in front of Ixor. "My name is King Hobart Victinours, king of this castle in the land of Tonest. What is your name."? The king asked. "My name is Ixor. Why was I brought here and for what reason?" said Ixor as he was filling his mouth with food.

Before answering, the king reached over the table to a goblet and a flask of wine, as he was pouring the wine he began to explain to Ixor about his father who apparently was the kings own brother, which made Ixor the king's Nephew. "Your father's name was Drago he died protecting the castle from the black knight, your mother died of a broken heart when he did not return to her." He said as he was drinking from the goblet.

"You were only two years old at that time, so I decided to foster you out to a woodman and his wife, It was only recently that I heard your foster mother died two years ago, I have never married so I had no way of looking after you, but now you are of an age I am ready to have you trained as a knight, only if you want to that is, or do you want to go back to the forest?"

Ixor thought for a moment then replied "Yes I would like to train as a knight what have I got to do?"

The king stroked the wine from his beard then answered. "It's not going to be easy for you it will be hard work to become a good knight but you should be used to that from working in the forest. Now it's time you rested for the night, tomorrow all will be shown to you." At that moment the king turned to the door and called out to his man servant to come and show Ixor to his bed chamber.

Chapter Two

The next day Ixor was awakened by the man he recognized from the day before, still smartly dressed, being of medium build and with a white beard that partly covered a scar down the left side of his face. “Up you get your training starts now.” This abrupt awakening was not what Ixor expected, but this person meant business. “Come with me now.” The man said, so Ixor followed, down to the court yard where he was placed in line with several other young men.

Looking straight at Ixor the man said. “My name is Ordmin I was your father’s man servant and now for as long as it takes I will teach you to become a knight, your father was the Red knight, we will try to make you as skilled with weapons as he was. Every morning you will always start with doing your daily chores which involves cleaning the stables, tending to the horses, cleaning and sharpening weapons and of course, most important of all, battle skills with the other students."

Ixor had always been used to hard work but this was going to be different to what he was used to, knowing the other students had all been training for some years and were experienced with weapons.

Ixor knew he would have to prove to them he too could be as good.

After that first day of initiation Ixor soon made friends with the other students, they realized he was quick to learn their fighting techniques which would help them become knights.

Over the next four years life was as hard for Ixor as the king said it would be, most of the time the students were kept apart from the king and the other knights, The king would watch Ixor's progress from a distance, The teacher "Ordmin" kept it that way, knowing it would let him find his own identity.

In those years at the castle Ixor's questions about his parents were answered, apparently his mother was of noble birth being the daughter of a lord from another shire. His father and mother fell in love against the wishes of her father, so they ran away together to hide. Her father sent the Black knight to bring her back, after three years he found them at castle Tonest.

It was outside this castle his father the Red knight fought the Black knight and lost, his mother was forced to return to her father where she died of a broken heart, she left Ixor behind at the castle Tonest knowing her father the Lord would have him killed. After hearing this story Ixor vowed he would avenge their deaths.

Now at the age of sixteen Ixor and three of the other students were summoned to the main hall where the king needed to see them.

On entering the hall sitting at the large table was the king with Ordmin to his right, and to his left sat Sir Bellingham the blue knight and Sir Raymond the yellow knight.

The four students stood in line in front of the large table, curious as to why they had been sent for.

"The four of you are to be sent away on a quest." The king said. He then turned to Ordman "Tell them what they need to do".

Ordman stroked at his beard and said "The four of you have now completed your training, so to become a knight you all have to complete a final test. When you all leave the castle you will be escorted by these two knights who will make sure you succeed in your quest, if you succeed you will come back here to be knighted.

If you fail in your quest you will be returned here to start serving as a squire," Then Ordman's eyes widened as he said. "Make sure you do not fail." With this remark which seemed like a warning Ordman went on to say. "You will all be taken to the armoury where you will take a sword and shield each, you will then be taken to separate destinations. You will then be told to recover an article at each place. Each article will aid you to obtain the book of knowledge at the last task. You will then bring it back here to the castle. Sir Bellingham and Sir Raymond will take each student to the place where they will complete their task. Each student must attempt their task on their own if you fail the next chosen student will try. All the tasks must be completed. The two knights must not help you in any way. You will then all return to the castle," ("If you survive that is.")

A shudder went through each student with that last remark. This was a test that was going to push them to their limits. Also their biggest problem was that none of them had a horse for this trip, it meant that they would have to walk there and back.

The two knights on their horses with the four students who were walking behind, were trying to keep up as they left the castle that day as they headed in the direction of the forest,

The other three students' names were Gerrard, Descond and Favour. Descond was tall, slim, with a sharp facial appearance and talked with a lisp, Gerrard was on the porky side with a fat round face and of medium height but well spoken, but Favour was Ixor's best friend who was very short in height, with long blond hair and with good looks to match. Over those long hard four years they had all relied on each other, they had always helped each other out of problems that they had encountered, so to stand back and watch each other in danger was going to be hard.

On reaching the forest they travelled on through which took all day. As the light began to diminish they decided to set up camp for the night at the far edge of the forest, where in the distance they could see a coppice in the middle of a field. Sir Bellingham leaned forward in his saddle and pointed "Tomorrow that's where the first task is to take place." He then looked down with a smirk at Gerrard and said "You Gerrard will be first in line then we will start to see what you are all capable of, so get a good night's sleep tonight you will all need it. Tomorrow we start off very early."

Chapter Three

Very early next morning the four students awoke to the smell of food and loud talking, the knights had been out hunting for food and were now cooking several rabbits on a spit over a fire. Sir Raymond called to the students. "Come and get some food, you are all going to need it, we don't know when we will eat again in the next few days."

After the meal they all gathered their belongings and weapons then started off in the direction of the coppice.

After reaching the coppice, inside amongst the trees was a large pit, where the knights dismounted from their horses, Sir Bellingham then looked at Gerrard and said. "You have to climb down into the pit then chop off the head of the 'Spiake' then bring it back up here to us then we can take the venom from its fangs." Gerrard said. "What's a Spiake?" "Look into the pit and you will see." Said Sir Raymond as they all started to look over the edge, There below amongst skeletons of animals and humans was a huge snake with a fury body of a spider, it had eight legs, its face was of a spider which had these large protruding fangs, it was about twenty foot in length, the colour was green and black. It lay there fast asleep it also looked as though it had just eaten which was good news for Gerrard. He then started to put his shield over his head and on to his back, he made sure his sword was easy for access from its scabbard, he then started to climb down some ivy branches that hung down the sides of the pit, Ixor said to the knights. "You cannot let him do this on his own he is too heavy for climbing down on that ivy. It doesn't look strong enough to hold him. He will be killed." All of a sudden the vine broke and Gerrard fell into the pit just in front of the Spiake. As Gerrard tried to stand up the spiake's eyes opened, it then attacked with a sudden thrust of its head its fangs imbedded into the side of Gerrard's body, with a loud scream from the pain just inflicted to his side Gerrard lifted his sword to strike but was shaken violently from side to side which made him lose his sword.

From the top of the pit they all looked down in horror, all of sudden Ixor dropped his shield and with his sword in his hand jumped into the pit and onto the body of the Spiake with an almighty strike he took the spiake's head off, Ixor fell from the beasts body and landed on to bones which covered the floor, with a thrust he put his sword through the mouth of the Spiake and between Gerrard's body to release the fangs from their grip. After this rush of adrenaline, Ixor knelt beside Gerrard who was already dying from the venom inside his body, it took only thirty seconds then Gerrard took his last breath. With tears in his eyes Ixor held Gerrard's head in his arms, placed his hand over his eyes and closed them.

After retrieving the body of Gerrard and the head of the Spiake from the pit Sir Bellingham said to Ixor. "You were not supposed to interfere in each of your tasks, but we will let you off just this once." With that sort of comment spoken at that time Ixor fumed back and replied. "I don't care we have just lost one of our friends and I have not forgotten the way in which you brought me to the castle those four years ago, tied up like an animal." Sir Bellingham replied "When you eventually become a knight you can call me out to a duel but at this time you are all here to do as you are told, now put the spiake's head on a log so that I can retrieve some venom from its fangs, then get the other students to make a pyre for Sir Gerrard as from this day he will be remembered as a knight."

After the cremation of Sir Gerrard the two knights and three remaining students headed off in the direction of some mountains. While they were travelling Sir Raymond explained to the students the next task. "At the foot of the mountains if you look up you will see a very large nest, in that nest are some eggs, it will be Favour's task to climb up and bring back one, but you have to avoid the vulcrom, its beak is full of needle sharp teeth it also has a twenty foot wing span which if it hits you can kill you, the only time to succeed is when it is away from its nest hunting." When Sir Raymond had finished explaining Favour looked around to Ixor and said. "Try not to help me if I get into difficulty I will do my best to get out of it I don't want you to get into any more fights with Sir Bellingham ok."Ixor looked fondly at his friend then said. "It does not matter, the problem between Sir Bellingham and myself, has been a long time coming, I will help you if I have to don't worry about it."

On reaching the base edge of the mountains they all looked up to see where the nest was. With his young keen eyes Descond with his lisp said. "There it ith, on that ledge, about forty feet up to the left of that big boulder." Sir Raymond replied, "Wait till we see the vulcrom fly from its nest, then Favour can start climbing, we do not want to lose another student if we can help it."

Suddenly there was an almighty whoosh above their heads, as the vulcrom flew to its nest with a sharp shrill from its beak "There it is now we must wait for it to fly away again." Sir Raymond said.

Ixor looked at Favour then said. "It's better to go now while the vulcrom is on its nest, by the time you get to the nest it would have flown again, also take this net to carry the egg in, you don't want to drop it on the way down." Favour took the hint then began to climb, when he reached halfway with the boulder just above his head that kept him out of the view of the vulcrom, suddenly there was another whoosh from its wings as it flew off, Favour now took the opportunity to quickly scale the boulder and reach the nest, he then found there were three eggs in the nest, he decided to only take one egg as he placed it into the net, then he tied the net around his neck with the egg hanging down his back, he made sure the sky was still clear then started to climb down the mountain, he just reached the others when all of a sudden that eerie shrill was heard again as the vulcrom swooped down between the two knight's horses, both horses reared throwing the two knights to the ground. Sir Raymond was thrown into some gorse bushes that gave him a soft landing, as for Sir Bellingham his fall was more dramatic he fell amongst rocks with a loud crack from inside his armour, as he was laying there writhing in agony the vulcrom flew around for another attack. Startled, the three students drew their swords ready, when out of nowhere appeared a knight on his horse with his shield and his lance pointing towards the vulcrom. As it dived towards everyone the lance penetrated right through the vulcrom's chest with the sound of a loud suction noise, the lance flew from the knight's gauntlet over his head then landed behind him with the vulcrom in a heap on the ground "dead."

Ixor recognised this knight from the colour of his plume as the green knight Sir Blades from his first encounter of knight's.

As Sir Bellingham laid there still in agony from breaking his arm, a cheer sounded for the demise of the vulcrom from everyone except Favour he alone knew there were two more eggs up there in the nest and no mother to tend for them, it saddened him greatly but he kept silent.

Sir Blades dismounted from his horse then with Sir Raymond went over to the fallen knight, lifting him to his feet Sir Blades said."I know an old healing man close by I will take Sir Bellingham there." They then removed his armour and put his arm in a crude splint so as to make him more comfortable for the journey next day.

After everyone explained their situations they camped for the night on a meal of bird meat filling their stomachs to the limit. The only person who did not eat any of the bird was Favour, The guilt of destroying the vulcrom which was the last of its kind, was something he could not forget' that's why during the night when everyone was asleep he disappeared for three hours, but that is another story for another time.

Chapter Four

Next morning there was a sweet smell from the gorse on the fire which was disguising a stench from a makeshift latrine on the out- skirts of the camp, everyone had severe stomach ache except Favour, "The vulcrom had made its last attack."

After recovering slightly the group packed up the camp, then made sure the egg was secure from damage, gathered their weapons and armour then set off around the mountain in the direction of a small building by a stream in the far distance. When they reached the building Sir Blades with the now fevered Sir Bellingham said goodbye to the group, knocked at the door then entered the building.

That left Sir Raymond with the three students to travel on to complete the next two tasks, as they travelled Sir Raymond said. "The next task will be for Descond." as he looked down at him from his horse. "We are heading towards the wet lands where there is a great swamp, there you will be asked to retrieve the spines from the back of a drillworm, the only way to succeed is to cover your body from top to toe with the clay from the swamp, you must not let them see you, if they do they will suck all of your blood from your body. The clay is the only substance they cannot see through."

Descond with his usual lisp asked "What doth a drillworm look like?" "It's a large slug with a huge suction mouth that it uses to cling onto its foes, it also has wings with sharp spines down its back." Sir Raymond replied.

As they travelled the land became softer under foot until they reached as far as they could go, in front of them was a barrier of swamp land. "This is where you cover yourself in clay you must make sure you do not leave any part of your body exposed." Sir Raymond said.

Descond undressed to his under garments then he got Ixor with Favour to smother himself all over with the clay, then he began to wade through knee high in mud, in the distance he could see flying beings diving in and out of the mud. "That could be them he thought." As he started to raise his sword he just remembered he had forgotten his shield. "Well it ith too late to go back now thethe drillwormth are diving jutht in front of me" he thought. Just as he was about to slice through one of the creatures he slipped into the mud where there was a pool of water which washed some of the mud from his body, As soon as that happened he found he was exposed to the drillworms, they started to dive upon his body, he stood no chance at the onslaught as they started to suck the blood in great quantities from his body.

The knight and his two students watched in awe from the edge of the swamp as they saw the life being taken from Descond's body, there was no time to save him, no one said a word. Fury took over in all their eyes as they began to cover themselves in clay. While Descond's body was being drained of all its blood the three warriors charged with their weapons raised high into the swamp killing as many of the drillworms as they could, the onslaught was so furious the rest of the drillworms disappeared into the mud.

When they eventually retrieved Descond's body with several spines from the drillworms, they buried Descond's drained body under a pile of rocks well away from the swamp. "Rest in peace Sir Descond," were the words spoken by Sir Raymond over his grave.

As the three of the remaining group left the low lands no one looked back. They were all sickened by what had just happened. It took the rest of the day before anyone would speak.

As they were approaching a river, there beside it was a small wood. Sir Raymond said. "We shall make camp for the night before the light fades. Tomorrow will be the task for Ixor. If you both look across the river you will see a group of hills, inside those hills are filled with catacombs. Somewhere inside them is the book of knowledge. There's one little problem though, there is this old hag called Pastazel who protects it. Many men have tried to possess the book and failed, their bodies are still in there somewhere." Before Ixor began to speak, Himself and Favour sat down for a rest from the days toil, both young men were exhausted. It was not long before curiosity got the better of him, he then said. "It can't be that hard to take a book from an old woman there's more to this than you are letting on to." Sir Raymond grinned slightly then said. "Yes you are right, this old woman as you call her has the power to paralyse anyone she happens to touch, it is a known fact she likes the taste of human flesh especially young men like you. The three items we gathered in the last few days are going to help you to destroy her. Tomorrow we will make a bow from willow taken from the wood, then the spines from the drillworms will make the arrows it's only these spines that can penetrate the old hags body nothing else can, the venom from the Spiake will be coated on the spines only that one item can kill her nothing else can." Sir Raymond then went on to say. "You will smother yourself all over with the yolk from the vulcrom's egg, only then will you be protected from the old hags touch. If you manage to obtain the book the king has advised me to tell you under no circumstances should you open the book." "Why not, what's the big secret?" Ixor Replied. Sir Raymond looked a little cross as to why this young student was questioning his instructions from the king. "All I know is something bad will happen if you do open it. Just do as the king asks."

Chapter Five

Next morning Ixor made his way into the wood to make the bow he needed for his task, making his way amongst the trees he came face to face with a grey haired old man dressed in rags who looked as though he could do with a good meal. "Not another young man ready to die for his king, my advice to you is to go home while you still can." The old man said. "Why should I." Ixor said reaching for his sword. The old man stood back behind a tree. "I'm not looking for trouble just trying to give you some good advice which might help keep you alive."The old man said as he hid from view. Ixor said. "Okay, what's on your mind?" The old man went on to tell Ixor that he, his wife and her sister lived in the wood happily for many years, until one day some gypsies passed by, the gypsies sold his wife a bottle of youth potion that was supposed to keep her young, she shared the bottle with her sister, only to find the potion had the reverse affect with both of them ageing quickly, they both became violent, their hunger for human flesh was apparent, his wife worried she might kill her husband she thought it best herself and her sister should move away. The old man sighed for a moment, he went on to say. I have always had the responsibility of being the keeper of the book of knowledge. They stole the book when they took off, hoping it could help them become normal again.

Listening to the old man's story made no difference to Ixor he was still going to fulfill his task, he told the old man he was sorry for his problems but he could not turn back now he must go on. The old man said. "Don't say I didn't warn you." He turned then disappeared into the wood.

While Ixor was away, Sir Raymond with his student Favour went about to prepare the spines which they dipped into the venom for the arrows, Ixor would need to see in the dark, so they also made a torch out of a large branch which they bound with rag soaked in bees wax.

When everything was ready, Ixor returned, he kept quiet about the old man, to the other's it was obvious that the skill of his early years that he spent in the forest had given him the experience to make the strongest of bows, he also brought back ten shafts for the spines to be attached to.

When all items that he needed were ready they packed up the camp then travelled across the river towards the hills. Just outside the entrance to the catacombs the egg was cracked over Ixor's head the messy yolk poured down all over his torso, Sir Raymond asked Favour to rub it in and make sure it covered the whole of his body. "Now you should be well protected from the old hag's touch." Favour said as he was wiping the yolk from his hands.

Sir Raymond said. "We will give you two hours in there, if you are not out in that time I will send in Favour to take your place." He lit the torch then fixed it to the front of Ixor's shield so that it would shine above and behind his head.

Ixor carefully placed the arrows through a funnel he had made earlier then fixed it to his belt which was specially made to protect the tips of the poisoned spines. He made sure his sword was easily accessible from his scabbard then his shield with the torch was secured to his back, "Now I am ready." He thought.

As he passed through the entrance to the catacombs the smell of rotting flesh was almost unbearable, a thought crossed his mind. "What have I let myself in for, will I get out of here alive." Trying to overcome his fears Ixor pressed on through the narrow tunnel that seemed to be taking him downhill. “Thank goodness there’s only one tunnel,” He thought.

The tunnel seemed to go on for a very long way then all of a sudden Ixor’s feet gave way, he found he was falling into a pit, with his natural instinct he put his bow across the top of pit to stop himself falling. Hanging in mid air he swung his legs up to the other side edge of the pit then lifted himself out. “That was close I’ll have to watch my step from now on.” He thought. As he looked back down into the pit the torch from behind his head lit up human remains from other unlucky souls who fell into the trap. Turning, he walked on cautiously he then approached a bend in the tunnel where he could see daylight ahead, when he came out of the tunnel he arrived into a large open circled area with walls one hundred feet high, in the walls four high were stone coffins. The smell down here was more intense than what it was at the entrance.

After adjusting his eyes to the light he then took his shield from his back, he removed the torch then dowsed it into the ground, looking around he noticed a large coffer situated against a wall underneath one of the coffins. There was no sign of the old hag Pastazel. With his bow now accompanied with an arrow he made his way over to look inside the coffer, as he was just about to lift the lid there was an almighty scream, out from the top of a coffin above Ixor's head was Pastazel, her eyes were full of fury as she launched herself in full flight at Ixor's throat, her fingers were extra long with sharp unforgiving nails as they began to grip his neck, the scream became louder as her hands began to burn from touching the yolk on Ixor's body, as she fell back in pain Ixor pulled his bow back then let fly one of his arrows which just missed her, he then took another arrow from his belt but was too late, because Pastazel's feet and legs were so long she was able to move faster than normal people.

Ixor had never seen anyone this ugly before, her breath stank and her teeth were black and jagged, she had long matted hair which covered her naked wrinkled body. Just as he was about to string his arrow Pastazel threw herself again at him, side stepping he shoved the arrow into her stomach, falling to her knees with her hands still burning she groaned in pain. In no time at all Ixor loaded his bow then fired at point blank range into her heart, making her to fall forward onto her face, with the arrow appearing out through her back, leaving nothing to chance he fired another arrow into the back of her neck, she lay there not moving, the old hag was dead.

"That was easier than I thought it was going to be, now where's that book of knowledge." He thought. He turned around to go over to the coffer. When out of nowhere there was another scream as an identical looking beast was attacking him. "She looks like Pastazel's twin, good job they didn't attack me together." He thought. She jumped in the air towards him with her hands hitting him in the chest. Ixor fell back on to the floor with the monster on top about to take a bite into his neck. Without hesitation he drew his sword, with a thrust he sent the point into her side, her hands were burning as she was sent with the sword in her side screaming across the ground. Standing up, Ixor grabbed his bow, loaded the arrow, firing it straight and true through the old hag's eye, his adrenaline was so high it created a power so intense that the arrow travelled out at the back of her head. Bending over her he took his sword out of her lifeless body, looking around he placed the sword back into its scabbard. He thought. "I hope that's the last of them this is beginning to wear me out."

Walking attentively over to the coffer he lifted the lid, inside was a large brown book without any inscription on its cover. "What's so different about this book?" he wondered. He was told not to look inside, the temptation was too much he opened it almost at once a great light hit his eyes sending him into a dream of being somewhere else. In front of him he could see a knight standing in front of the king, in full armour. The knight had a shield which displayed the crest of a bat in full flight. The plume from his helmet was black.

Standing in the centre of a clearing surrounded with trees the king was pointing back over the trees towards the castle Tonest. The vision changed all of a sudden Ixor was now seeing a battle outside the castle. It was his father, the red knight, dueling with the Black Knight. He watched his father lose. The vision changed again, this time he saw a lady being dragged away from the castle by the Black Knight with the king and Ordmin his teacher, watching from the ramparts. The knight lifted her across his saddle climbed upon his horse then rode off towards the forest. Again the vision changed. This time he watched his teacher Ordmin deliver a small child into the arms of his step mother who was standing amongst the trees in the forest he grew up in.

The light from the book faded as did the images. Awakened from his trance Ixor began to have doubts of the king's sincerity. He wondered "Did he send me here to be killed. What would he gain from my demise?" These questions bothered Ixor greatly, he knew in his heart he would have to get to the truth when he got back to the castle. Closing the book he secured it onto his belt, gathered up his weapon's, lit the torch then made his way back through the tunnel. "His task completed."

The light was harsh again on Ixor's eyes when he appeared out from the tunnel. The touch of cold metal pressed against his throat was a surprise he did not expect. "If you value your life you'll hand the book over." Was the words spoken into his ears from behind. He took the book from his belt then passed it over his shoulder. The sharp pain with a flash of light was the last thing he remembered. He eventually awoke from his concussed stupor. Over by a tree in full view was Sir Raymond and Favour tied up back to back. Their voices were muffled from under the rags tied around their mouths. Recovering from the blow to his head Ixor released the knight and his friend. "Who was it that attacked us?" Ixor asked, while he was untying their hands. Sir Raymond said, "The Black Knight. He surprised us both, tied us up then waited for you to come out of the tunnel." "How did he know we were after the book of knowledge, someone must have told him, who else would have known?" Ixor asked. Sir Raymond thought for some time then replied. "It could have been any number of people, who knows, we may never know. For now you need cleaning up, you don't look too good. Come on over to the river then we can clean the blood from your head wound also let's wash of that egg from your body it's beginning to stink."

After a clean, Ixor said. "We need to get that book back or there's no chance I will become a knight, did either of you see which direction he rode off in?" "Over there towards the forest, between those two large trees." Favour said, as he pointed towards that direction."

Sir Raymond said. "You will have to retrieve it on your own. It's still your task. We can't help you. I will give you two days to complete it. We shall see you at that building where Sir Bellingham is recovering. If you do not return in two days we shall return to the castle without you. I will let you take my horse. Make sure you look after him. Good luck and try to stay alive.

Picking up his shield with his bow, Ixor climbed onto Sir Raymond's horse, he then headed off in the direction of the forest. "It's time to sort out once and for all this so called Black Knight." He thought.

Favour waved goodbye to his friend as he disappeared from view through the trees. "This could be the last time I'll ever see him." He thought.

Chapter Six

The day was almost over when Ixor reached the far side of the forest, the light was almost gone as he made camp for the night. His head was still thumping from the blow he took earlier. "With a good night's sleep I should feel better in the morning." He thought. After he had put his horse out to pasture he settled down under a tree for the night.

Feeling better Ixor awakened to the sound of birds. He quickly gathered his belongings. Saddled his horse then rode off down into a large valley where in the distance he could see a small one man marquee. As he got closer he noticed the shield displayed outside. "It's the Black Knight; I've caught up with him already, now at last it's time to repay him for all his wrong doings. I'll call him out to fight." Ixor thought.

The young warrior rode straight and fast towards the shield, drawing his sword he hit it hard' knocking it from its pedestal sending it with a clang to the floor. "Come out and fight you murdering coward, this day is your last." Ixor shouted.

Helmet in hand a seven foot giant emerged from the marquee. "Go away boy you are not man enough to take me on, go back to your nursery before you do something that you'll regret." He said putting on his helmet and picking up his shield.

The sight of this huge man would put anyone off, let alone call him out for a fight. His square jaw matched his body stature; Large and frightening. The arms and legs of this giant were like tree trunks.

That last statement from the knight's mouth sent a rage through Ixor's body like no other. "It was you who killed my parents, now prepare to die you dog." Ixor said as he jumped from his horse with his sword and shield. He then attacked the knight full on with a thrust to the chest. The shield from the knight parried the blow then the knight turned it and pushed the shield forward knocking Ixor to the floor. Turning the shield on its edge the knight sat on Ixor with it against his throat. Ixor's hands were now pinned to the ground. He was unable to move with this heavyweight on his chest. The knight then said. “It’s not of my doing that killed your parents. I was pawn for the kings bidding. We all have to obey him. I still regret to this day when I killed your father. The king wanted you to die as well, he thought the best time for you to be killed would be on your quest, he sent me to make sure, but I only kill in battle not in cold blood. I’ll tell you the truth about your mother and father. Only if you promise to stop attacking me, only then will I let you up?” Ixor nodded and said. “Yes I will, only if you stop treating me like a boy.”

The Black Knight cautiously let Ixor get to his feet. He need not have worried Ixor was true to his word.

The marquee was the place that day the two adversaries made their peace. Sitting opposite each other the knight started to explain the true story of Ixor’s parents.

Apparently Ixor’s father was the oldest son of the original king, Ixor’s grandfather. His own father the Red Knight preferred to explore and travel the land looking for excitement which kept him away for at least seven years. Then the old king died and with his absence his younger brother Hobart stole the title to become the new king.

While he was away his father the Red Knight met his mother Lady Silvianda, who against her father's wishes decided to run away to live together, that's when Ixor arrived into the world.

It was King Hobart who instructed the Black Knight to track down and kill Ixor's father, it was not his mother's father who is Lord Darnley. He had nothing to do with it. The black knight went on to say he had no idea the chase would take himself back to the castle, that's when he called Ixor's father to a duel outside the castle, after he had killed the Red Knight the King instructed the Black Knight to return Ixor's mother back to Lord Darnley her father without her child, the king had other dark plans for Ixor.

Everything started to make sense to Ixor. "Why did he separate me from my mother?" Ixor asked. The Black Knight said. "I don't know you will have to ask Ordmin he was the person who took you to the woodman and his wife' I think the king told Ordman to get rid of you. But Ordman could not kill you. That's why you ended up at the woodman's cottage."

"Why does he want the book of knowledge?" Ixor asked.

"Now that's a puzzle to me, all I know is he was hoping that you would fail in your task, he did not know which task the knight's would pick for you, only that any one of the tasks would be your undoing, then he would have been rid of you for good."

Standing up the Black Knight started to look uncomfortable, walking backwards and forwards he went on to say. "I have something else to tell you, you probably will not like what I have to say, but I have to get it off my chest. Your mother is still alive. I married her two years after your father died. That's another reason why I could not kill you, you are my stepson. Your mother still thinks you are dead."

Ixor's mouth opened wide in disbelief at what he had just heard. He sat there for while until it had sunk in then said. "You mean you have kept this secret all these years and not told anyone, why tell me now, what am I supposed to do about it?

"I know you are angry, but I would like to take you to see your mother if you'd let me that is, then you could meet your grandfather Lord Darnley, who allowed me to become part of his family. You'll find him a kind and gentle lord, especially to his people and the garrison he runs, so what do you say will you come?" The Knight said.

Again Ixor was astonished at what he had just heard, he sat there for a while, then curiosity got the better of him, he then said. "Yes ok. How far is it to the garrison and will my mother accept me as her lost son or will I cause a problem?"

The knight now looked at Ixor with softer eyes then said. "I don't really know we'll have to take it as it comes ok? Oh by the way you can call me Sir Endevoure if you want or father it's up to you."

"I'll just call you sir for now if you don't mind." Ixor answered.

That day the two would be enemies got to become friends as they sat eating and talking about the past and the future. It was in the afternoon they mounted their horses then rode off towards the Lord's garrison, leaving the marquee still standing for another day.

Chapter Seven

Riding for many miles the two comrades eventually came into view of the garrison. The outer walls reached ten foot high. The two main gates were made of thick solid oak spanning twelve foot across. Inside was a large settlement of houses which surrounded the large manor house.

With their mounts both riders made their way down the hill towards the complex. Sir Endevoure, pointing to the manor said. "That's where your mother and grandfather live. When we get there let me do the talking, I'll try and smooth the way for you, allow me to get them over the shock of meeting you."

Ixor agreed it was going to be just as difficult for him as it was for them.

On reaching the gates of the garrison the guards allowed them to pass through as they recognized Sir Endevoure, passing on through the houses Ixor noticed how happy all the people were. The adults and children kept waving at Sir Endevoure, he waved back it was obvious there was a fondness between the knight and the people of this community.

Approaching the manor in full view of the two travelers stood on the front steps a tall dark haired woman. Her clothes were of the finest silks you could find. For her age she still had the looks you could yearn for. This was Ixor's mother Lady Silvianda.

Sir Endevoure waved to his wife before he dismounted with Ixor from their horses. Two servants appeared to take their steeds off to the stables and bed them down for the night.

Moving over to his wife the knight gave her an embracing kiss then told her he had brought her a surprise as he beckoned Ixor to come forward. "This is your son you lost all those years ago, his name is Ixor."

Looking at each other the recognition was apparent. "My son" Was the words Lady Silvianda said as she held her arms out for an embrace from Ixor. The response was without hesitation. Ixor held his mother again after fourteen years.

"Where's your father, I thought he would be out here with you?" The knight said to his wife.

Releasing her hold on Ixor, Lady Silvianda turned to her husband and said. "He's in bed, he has not been well these last few days, I don't think he has long to live. Let me take Ixor to see him before he dies?"

"Oh come on he's been dying for years, you know and I know he's as strong as an ox, come on we'll all go together to see him. Let's try and cheer him up." Sir Endevoure said as he took his wife's hand then walked her towards the front door with Ixor following behind.

The knight his wife with her son walked through the corridors amongst the servants who were busy with their daily duties. They arrived at the door of the Lord's bedroom chamber. Lady Silvianda knocked at the door as she called out "It's only me." Then she let herself in. "Are you decent I have brought you a surprise." She said.

The shock on what they viewed on entering was too embarrassing for Lady Silvianda. On his bed stark naked with a servant woman, enjoying the fruits of life was Lord Darnley. "Oh no!" was her response as she back stepped into the corridor, shutting the door quick. Ixor laughed to himself at what he had just seen. "At least the old man is human." He said trying not laugh out loud.

"We'll come back later when he's more decent, looks as though he's not dying after all." Lady Silvianda said with her face reddening.

Later Ixor did meet his grandfather together they toured the manor and its grounds. Ixor was impressed on how well liked the lord was by his servants and the people within the community, everywhere he would receive a wave with a smile.

That evening in the great hall at the manor a feast was prepared for Ixor in honour of his return to his mother. Large tables surrounded the perimeter of the hall, where all the important dignitaries of the community were sitting. Lord Darnley now recovered from his orgy, sat at the head of the tables with his daughter on his right, Ixor and Lord Endevoure on his left. The old lord with greying long hair and beard still had the good looks of a man ten years his junior, stood up to make a toast to his grandson's home coming. "This toast is for my grandson and your future king." Everyone stood up then raised their glasses towards Ixor. "Long live our future king." The response was immediate from everyone.

To Ixor this was a complete surprise let alone something he had never contemplated. He turned to Sir Endeavour and said. "The thought of me being the future king had never entered my head, can this be true?" Sitting down the knight whispered in Ixor's ear. "Yes you are the rightful heir to the throne you are your father's son Prince Ixor Victinours of Tonest, anyway when I took the book of knowledge from you looking in it I watched you being crowned. You will be the king one day I swear it on my life."

Ixor said. "Before I can even think of being a king I must return tomorrow to the castle with that book otherwise I will never become a knight."

Sir Endevoure laughed. "You don't have to worry about being knighted you inherit your father's title. No other person can bestow a knighthood on you except yourself. You are the red knight. Now we must increase your training and make you a force to be reckoned with." The lord butted in on the conversation. "We have your father's armour here for you, your mother asked for it to be returned here with his body, he is buried in our personal graveyard, we will take you there later after dinner."

Changing the subject the lord went on to say. "We must find you a wife while you are here. You'll need an heir to succeed you for the future." With a disapproving look there was "Ah-hmm," from Lady Silvianda. "Now that's enough of that father there's plenty of time for such things Ixor will have enough to do without marrying him off."

That evening Lord Darnley introduced Ixor to many dignitaries and their daughters, none of the young ladies interested him, most were either too fat or too thin with no brains, any way he was more interested in going outside to look at his father's grave. The air in the hall was getting stuffy, Ixor made that as his excuse to leave.

Outside with his mother, Sir Endeavour and his grandfather, Ixor was taken to the graveyard. Standing in front of his father's grave a tear appeared from his eye. The sight of the stone dragon perched on top of the head stone with the words. "HERE LIES DRAGO VICTINOURS KNIGHT OF THE DRAGON RED. VALIANT TO THE END." was too emotional for him.

Thoughts of what the future would bring were now running through Ixor's head, he turned to the knight. "Where's the book of knowledge I would like to look inside it. You never know it might show us the future."

"You can look if you like but the book of knowledge has now been hidden by Lord Darnley only he knows where it is, anyway I already know your future I told you I looked earlier and have seen you being crowned. Only now you need to concentrate on your extra fighting skills that I will be teaching you. And that starts tomorrow." Was the reply from Sir Endevoure.

Chapter Eight

Next day Sir Endevoure supplied Ixor with his father's armour and sword. The crest on the shield displayed the red dragon and from the top of the helmet a red plume. This was the first time Ixor had tried on full armour, finding it heavy and clumsy he said to the knight. "How am I supposed to fight in this, it's so clumsy trying to move around."

Reaching out to catch his young warrior Sir Endevoure said. "That's why you must do this extra training to get you used to moving around in full armour when different situations happen to arise. Over the next few months we shall train you to be a force for the future to be reckoned with. First you'll learn to fight on the ground then joust from your horse. Only when I think your training is complete will I allow you to go back and face the king."

During the following days Ixor noticed how much defense training and fighting the people of the garrison were doing. It was the Lord's policy that every able-bodied male should hold his own from an attack on the garrison.

Days turned into weeks then years as did the boy who became a man. Then one day when Ixor was battling with swords in the training ground against his stepfather the Black knight. The alarm was raised from the guards at the gates. Outside approaching the garrison, a lonely knight on his horse with the crest of a dove displayed upon his shield, with a white plum from his helmet. Stopped at the gates and asked to speak to Lord Darnley.

Being allowed in the knight dismounted from his almost white horse. Looking over at this knight, Ixor recognized his old friend Favour. "Favour why have you come here?" He shouted as he ran towards his long lost friend. Both men held each other in a manly embrace. "I've missed you. I see you have been knighted. Why did the king make you a white knight? It's so bland." Ixor said in his excitement.

"The king thought me to be a little too gentle for a knight, so he bestowed upon me the white dove of peace as my crest, I am now known as Sir Favour the white knight. Anyway what are you doing here we all thought you had been killed on that day you did not arrive back at the healers place. Sir Raymond was very upset on losing his horse." Sir Favour laughed as he went on to say. "He has not found another one to match it. He keeps falling off his new horses."

Looking sternly at the two youngsters Sir Endevoure shout's out. "Ixor you have not finished your daily training yet, come on let's get on with it." "I thought you and the black knight were enemies." Sir Favour said when seeing the man who had tied him together with Sir Raymond outside the catacomb. "It's a long story I can't stop to tell you now I'll tell you later after my training session." Ixor said while running back over towards the despondent knight.

Two of the guards escorted Sir Favour to the manor. Inside the great hall he faced Lord Darnley and Lady Silvianda sitting beside each other at a large table. The lord said. "What can we do for you sir knight." "My name is Sir Favour I have been sent here from the king to ask you to supply a few men to accompany me on a mission to rescue a princess, who was kidnapped last week by ruffians while travelling on a road through a forest near to here."

Lord Darnley was a wise and clever man he knew there was more to this that met the eye somehow he knew the king would have a hidden agenda. “What’s in it for me if I help the king?” The lord said.

“I don’t really know he just asked me to ask you, all I can think of is he would help you if you needed it some time. This princess with a large dowry was betrothed to the king by her own father king Plestoe from a faraway land across the seas. I got the impression the king would like Sir Endevoure to help without actually asking him.” The young knight said.

The mention of a woman to the lord interested him deeply “I wonder if we can find a suitor for Ixor.” He thought. He went on to say. “What is the lady’s name?” Sir Favour replied. “Princess Collester.”

Turning to lady Silvianda the lord said. “Would you mind if I sent your husband on this mission?” She replied. “No I don’t but only if Ixor goes with him.” “Very well” Said the lord, looking back at Sir Favour he said. You’ll stay here for the night we’ll all have a meal, you must have lot’s to talk about with Ixor I believe he’s your friend.”

That evening another lavish meal was bestowed upon all those who attended. The knight’s got to know one another that night over many pitchers of ale from which they eventually staggered off into their own beds.

Next day with their heads thumping from the night before the knight's on their horses said their goodbyes as they made their way with the best six soldiers the lord could find, out through the gates of the garrison to the forest where Lady Collester was being held.

Two hours later on the outskirts of the forest Sir Endevoure told the other warrior's to keep their eyes open now that they were entering the forest. Following the rough road for about a mile they could see carrion flying ahead. Sir Endevoure told the others to wait until he had scouted ahead in the forest to see where the enemy was holding the princess.

Following the rough road for five minutes he came upon a sight of carnage, in front about twenty men lay butchered upon the ground, most of them with arrows protruding from their bodies. The smell was rank from the corpses making them attractive to carrion. "What kind of animal would leave the dead lying around and not bury them." He thought. Suddenly out of the forest there was a cry of help with screaming as though someone was being tortured. Making his way over a mound and through the trees towards the screams Sir Endevoure hidden from view behind a tree watched in horror the sight of a man tied to a tree being skinned alive by two barbarians. Standing and watching were thirty onlookers laughing and joking. Sickened at the sight beholding his eyes, the knight moved around silently towards the back of a makeshift hut placed to the rear of the group. Lifting some branches he glanced inside. There on the floor with a muddy face was the prettiest girl he had ever seen. Her hair was long and black that glistened like silver, her feature's small like a pixie with lips as red as a rose. The rope tied around her sank into beautifully formed body. "This young lady must be the princess." He thought. Creeping underneath the branches and into the hut the knight told her to be quiet by placing his finger to his lips. With a knife he began to cut through her bonds, after her release the knight guided her through the hole to the outside.

Just as they stepped outside a gruff voice spoke.

"You are a big fellow, thought you would get away with our bit on the side did you." Said one of the two pox faced, scruffy looking morons standing there in front of the knight. The princess fell to the ground in despair. Sir Endevoure drew his sword. Two swipes of the blade severed the head from the shoulders of one rogue then the arm from the other. The other rogue's end came with blood squirting from the thrust of the sword which penetrated to the hilt straight through into his stomach. Taking his sword out of the motionless body the knight took hold of the princess while at the same time sheathing his sword back into his scabbard.

The noise of the fight alerted the other barbarians who started to charge towards Sir Endevoure and the princess.

"Attack and kill the swine." Was the unexpected recognizable sound of Ixor as he and his men charged from all directions towards their adversaries It did not matter that they were outnumbered the fury of the attack with the surprise took the barbarian's of their guard. With half their men annihilated the barbarian's took flight. Wiping the blood from their swords Sir Favour with the men started to collect the bodies for burial.

Walking over to Sir Endevoure, Ixor said. "Good job we got here when we did otherwise you'd be dead." Ixor attention was suddenly drawn towards the princess he had never seen a girl who looked so pretty, "You must be princess Collesta, have you been hurt or would you like any help?" She was just about to reply when Sir Endevoure interrupted. "Of course the princess is fine just a little bruised that's all. Go and cut that poor soul down from the stake over there the sight of him is upsetting her highness."

It was that suggestion brought the princess to her senses as she said, "Yes please cut him down, he was my advisor and manservant he did not deserve such a horrid death, I'll miss him deeply."

When all the corpses from both sites were buried the princess later explained how her escort was surprised and how the dowry with the coach she was travelling in was taken away earlier by several of the thieves, leaving herself and her manservant to their fate with the rest of the gang.

"Without my dowry the king will not even consider marriage, I cannot return to my father, I have let him down, I am not worthy as a daughter." The princess said as she started to weep.

Taking them to one side Sir Endevoure planned with Ixor and Sir Favour their next move as he said. "Sir Favour with four of our men will accompany the princess back to the garrison. Ixor with myself and the other two men shall follow the trail of the coach. Let's hope we succeed there'll be no turning back."

From his first sighting of the princess, Ixor was smitten with love. He would go to the ends of the earth for her affections. The only problem was she was betrothed to the king. Would she even know how she affected him, these thoughts would help him to get through the next few days.

After both groups parted, Sir Endevoure with his band of warrior's on their horses travelled through the forest for some distance until they reached a bend in the track, suddenly arrows reigned overhead. With an arrow spearing one of their men through his neck killing him on the spot the rest of the group immediately jumped from their horses. Taking cover behind some of the trees Sir Endevoure said to Ixor. "I'll keep them occupied while you take the other soldier and creep around to their rear." Just as he had finished talking he sprang to his feet then started to run from tree to tree. With the arrows now aimed at the knight, Ixor with his man were able to crawl up a small hill towards the archers then made their way around to the rear of their adversaries.

Ixor counted six archers hidden in amongst the bushes which surrounded the trees. Whispering to his comrade he said. "You take the three on the right, I'll take the other three further over to the left." Both men crawled forward with their knives then started to clinically and methodically slit the throats of all the archers.

Making sure all was clear Ixor called out to Sir Endevoure. "Over here the coach is the other side of the hill in a clearing the horses are still with it." The three carefully walked towards the coach. Opening the door they found the dowry intact, two chests full of coins and jewels. "Now that's what you call a dowry Collesta's father must be very rich to offer all that wealth with his daughter, no wonder king Hobart is keen to marry her." The knight said.

Replying Ixor said. "Yes the alliance would make him very powerful too."

Just as they started to relax a twig snapped from behind the other side of the coach, a barbarian was hiding then started to make a run for it. Taking his sword from its scabbard, Sir Endevoure threw it with all his might. The sword caught the barbarian between the shoulder blades "I hope that's the last of them." The knight said while catching his breath.

After the burials of the enemy they placed their dead comrade inside the coach. Ixor, Sir Endevoure and the remaining soldier with the coach and all the horses began there long trip back to the garrison.

Chapter Nine

On arriving at the garrison Sir Favour with Princess Collesta were greeted with cheers from people lining the streets as they made their way to the manor house.

On arriving at the manor Sir Favour introduced princess Collesta to Lord Darnley who was standing there outside with Lady Silvianda to welcome her.

Sir Favour explained to the lord why only half of their numbers had returned he also told Lady Silvianda not to worry Ixor and Sir Endevoure would be back as soon as they had recovered the dowry coach.

Lady Silvianda soon made the princess feel at home joking and laughing they started to become friends.

That night now feeling relaxed with a hearty meal the princess was shown to her bed chamber, before entering the room she asked Lady Silvianda was the king nice and was he a good man because she had never ever seen him and did not know what to expect. “You mean you have never met the king, do realize he is a lot older than you. I thought your father would have told you before you left home.” Lady Silvianda said.

Princess Collesta’s mouth opened wide she thought she was being married to someone who was of the same age. “Oh I don’t know what I should do.” She said bursting into tears.

Placing her arms around the princess Lady Silvianda thought of an idea that would give the princess a chance to make her own mind up. “When Sir Favour takes you to the king, I’ll send my husband the black knight along to accompany you, if you decide you do not want to go through with it he’ll have a talk with the king to see if he will let you go, then he’ll try to bring you back if he can.” She said.

“Is your husband the knight who rescued me from the hut, if it is I know he’ll look after me?” The princess said wiping her eyes.

Helping the princess into her room lady Silvianda replied. “Yes he is. He has helped the king in the past if anyone can persuade him to let you off the marriage my husband can."

Early next morning the princess was wakened with cheers from outside her window, leaping from her bed she looked out through the window to see the dowry coach entering the garrison with Sir Endevoure, Ixor and the soldier. "Good they made it back I must go and thank them for saving my dowry." She thought.

A quick wash then dressed the princess rushed to join Lord Darnley with Lady Silvianda at the entrance of the manor to welcome back the three conquerors. When the lord and his daughter had finished their congratulating the princess stepped forward to give a kiss on the cheek of all three of her champions. "Thank you I will never know how I shall repay you." She said.

Ixor quickly answered for the three proud warriors. "It was nothing we only did what was right at the time." He then took the princess to one side and asked her. "After I have eaten then rested would you like to walk with me this afternoon I have something private to say to you?" Blushing, the princess was taken by surprise at Ixor's forwardness. She said. "Do you realize you are talking to a princess I have never had anyone try to ask me on a date before." Looking into her eyes and taking hold of her hand Ixor said. "One day I shall be a king, my father was the older brother to the king you are betrothed to, that throne should be mine by rights." Princess Collesta thought to herself. "Is this man for real I must find out if it is true," She said to Ixor. "Yes I will as long as you behave yourself?" "Of cause I will I would not have it any other way," was the reply.

That afternoon walking and talking together Ixor explained to the princess his true feelings towards her. It turned out the princesses feelings were starting to warm towards Ixor, it looked as though they had a lot in common. Now they had a problem on how the princess could avoid the marriage to the king. Talking for some time they decided to go along with lady Silvianda's idea. Darkness soon came that night as they cuddled together to keep each other warm.

The next day Lord Darnley agreed to let the princess stay for a few days. His excuse was to give her time to recover from her ordeal. Only the real truth was he wanted Ixor to enhance his love towards her, he could see the love they had for each other.

A week passed, Sir Endevoure had agreed to escort the princess to the king. Regrettably Ixor had agreed to let her go after talking it through with the knights. They decided Ixor should wait four days, if there was no news either way he would go to the castle to find out for himself. He thought. “Let’s hope the princess can find a way of returning to me.”

The dreaded day arrived when the coach and its escort were ready to depart from the garrison. Two soldiers driving the coach with the princess inside accompanied on their horses Sir Endevoure and Sir Favour made their way through the gates of the garrison to the outside.

With the princess now gone Ixor decided to train extra hard with the four hundred hardened soldiers the lord had. He knew one day he would have to rely on these men.

Chapter Ten

The coach with its party emerged from the forest to the outskirts of the castle walls. Outside jousting were many knights amongst them were Sir Raymond the yellow knight, Sir Blades the green knight and Sir Bellingham the blue knight who seemed to have recovered from the broken arm he had received years ago.

The knights when seeing the coach stopped their battling to escort the princess and her party through the castle gates.

It was obvious to Sir Favour there was no love between Sir Endevoure and the other three knights the looks said it all.

Entering the court yard everyone was met by either servants or squires. There on the steps by the main door was Ordmin waiting to escort the princess to her maids who would prepare her for the meeting of the king. Ordmin said to Sir Endevoure. “Did you recover the princess’s dowry.” Sir Endevoure said. “Yes we did but not without a fight and losing one good man.” Ordman with a little compassion said. “I’m sorry for the loss but the king wants to see you and Favour immediately in the main hall Sir Bellingham will escort you.”

They entered the main hall as usual the king was sitting at the head of the large table with a guard either side of him, many other guards stood with weapons at the ready around the hall.

The king looking confident with the amount of protection surrounding him gave a nod to some of the guards nearest Sir Endevoure. All at once they raised their swords towards the knight. Now prisoner Sir Bellingham removed Sir Endevoure’s sword from its scabbard. At the same time he told Sir Favour to leave the hall this was not his concern and the king would see him later. Sir Favour was outnumbered he thought the best thing to do was to leave which he did.

The king looking at the knight said. “You thought you could keep the secret of not killing Ixor from me well you were wrong these secrets have ways of reaching my ears, for not carrying out my orders you will be imprisoned until I decide what to do with you."

Sir Endevoure now looking cross at being made prisoner said. "But I saved the princess for you surely that would put things right and be in my favour."

"Ahh that little ruse you fell for it. Do you realize apart from wanting to marry the princess knowing it would create an alliance with her father, I took the opportunity to employ those rascals to kidnap her. I sent Sir Favour to you to help rescue her. It was only a matter of time before you would return here. Let's hope Ixor comes to save you." The king then pointed to the door. "Take him to the dungeons." The guards grabbed Sir Endevoure then marched him through the door to the dungeons.

Turning to Sir Bellingham the king said. "I would now like to see Sir Favour bring him to me."

Arriving back in the main hall Sir Favour said. "Your majesty what have you done with Sir Endevoure."

The king now looking pleased with himself said. "He is my prisoner, I now want you to go back to Ixor then tell him from me I will only release the knight if he was to give himself up to me.

Sir Favour now realised how devious the king was and that he had been used as a puppet, after this last errand he would never again do the kings bidding he would now side with his friend Ixor. Before leaving the castle Sir Favour visited his old teacher Ordmin. Over the last few years Sir Favour had always confided with him as someone he could trust. He told him of the king's intentions also he asked him to inform the princess of what was happening.

It took all that day for Sir Favour with the two soldiers to arrive back at the garrison. As the darkness of the night began to draw in they were allowed to pass through the gates then headed towards the manor.

Ixor on hearing of their return had rushed to the entrance hoping to see his princess again. "Where is she?" He shouted.

"I'm sorry Ixor the king has double crossed us he has imprisoned Sir Endevoure while holding onto the princess." He said as he dismounted from his horse.

Ixor now looking confused said. “Why has he done that I thought Sir Endevoure was the king’s champion?”

“Not any more, not since he did not complete the assassination of you. He has sent me to tell you he will release him only if you give yourself up to him.” Sir Favour went on to say. “The king used the circumstances of the princess to get to you. What will you do now?”

Just as he was about to reply Lady Silvianda appeared “What’s all this noise my father is trying to sleep. Sir Favour you have returned where’s my husband is he not with you?”

“No the king is holding him in prison he will only release him if Ixor gives himself up as an exchange.” The knight said.

Raged with fury Ixor called to a squire to fetch his armour, he was in that frame of mind that would make him leave and act immediately.

Stepping in front of Ixor with her hand beckoning for him to stop Lady Silvianda said. “Ixor don’t be so impetuous you need time to plan, you need to gather an army you cannot go on your own you must show you mean business by having a force behind you."

Suddenly Lord Darnley appeared. "Your mother is right I will deploy my soldiers immediately. Besides this is what they have all been trained for, to help you take your place as king."

Two hours later that night Ixor upon his horse dressed in the armour of the red knight ahead of three hundred well armed men left in the dark from the garrison. The army was made up of sixty archers who were all marksmen, one hundred and twenty men on horses armed with lances, with the other one hundred and twenty as infantry carrying swords and shields. Lord Darnley decided Sir Favour should stay behind with one hundred men to guard the settlement against any other invaders.

Four hours later reaching beyond the forest the army of Ixor positioned themselves out of reach around the perimeter of the castle. As it was dark they decided to set up camp until daylight.

During the night Ixor with his commanders discussed tactics for the days ahead, food and water was plenty so it was decided that they should lay siege for a few days hoping the enemy would be forced into submission.

Outnumbered two to one the troops ordered by the king stood in expectation in and around the battlements ready for the onslaught that was about to come, but nothing came.

Chapter Eleven

The next day Ixor positioned his archers to aim at the battlements around the castle. With this protection Ixor sent a courier who approached the drawbridge with ten of his horsemen. Shouting out loud he bellowed. "I have a message for the king ask him to send someone out to collect it."

For five minutes there was silence then suddenly the drawbridge was lowered. From out of the castle on horses appeared Ordmin with Sir Raymond, the knight in full battle armour with his visor down looked ready for battle as they rode up to the courier. Ordmin being a little unsteady on a horse for his age said. "Before you give me the message the king has instructed me to tell the Red Knight if he does not give himself up to the king, Sir Endevoure will be thrown from the battlements."

"I think you had better look at the message first." The courier said handing it over.

Taking the parchment Ordmin read it out loud so the knight beside him could hear. It read. "I Ixor Victinours son of Drago Victinours declare to be the rightful heir to the throne of lands and its castle of Tonest I am here to reclaim my property with the sacking of my uncle King Hobart Victinours." Signed :- Knight of the Dragon Red.

As soon as Ordmin had finished reading the courier went on to say. "Also my master has asked for the immediate release of the princess and Sir Endevoure he would then be prepared to fight the king in combat for the throne. If he does not comply the siege of the castle starts now."

Nothing more was to be said as both parties returned to their appropriate sides. The draw bridge closed behind Ordmin with his knight as they entered the castle.

At the great hall inside the castle the king was furious. "How dare this upstart preach to me I'll have his head spiked on a skewer," He screamed.

Ordmin was now worried at what the king would do next so he decided to come up with a plan that would sort out once and for all the realm that he had served for so long.

"Sire I have an idea that would solve all our problems, we could run a jousting tournament outside the castle walls. We have more knights than they have, even if we released Sir Endevoure we would still have the advantage. Whatever side wins takes the crown. Whoever loses shall be banished from the realm."

The king sat there in deep thought before saying. "Yes it's a good idea but we'll keep hold of the princess, there's no need to let her go, anyway I might lose her dowry we don't want that to happen do we." Pausing for a while the king then went on to say. "Send Sir Bellingham to me then you can organize the release of Sir Endevoure make sure he is escorted from the castle we don't want him to try anything."

While Ordmin was down by the dungeons arranging the release of Sir Endevoure the king was plotting a plan with the blue knight that could lead to the outsmarting and then the assassination of Ixor.

The gate's of the cell clanged open there sitting on the floor in amongst the filth was Sir Endevoure with his head buried in his hands. Looking up, Ordmin could see the knight had taken a beating from the other knight's. "Can you stand?" Ordmin asked.

Struggling to his feet the knight said. "Of cause I can, you don't think a beating would keep me down did you. It just gives me more reasons to fight back against the king and his followers. Anyway what do you want or have you just come to gloat."

Walking into the cell with his hand out to support the knight's weight, helping him up Ordmin said. "Certainly not I know there's no friendship between us from when you killed my master Sir Drago all those years ago, but we both have the same aims now that is to place the rightful heir to the throne. The king has promised your safe release after I persuaded him to arrange a tournament outside the castle between yourself and the other knights. The winning side would lay claim to the throne."

"You don't think he will keep his promise do you, he's likely to double cross everyone for his own gains." Sir Endevoure said while pushing away the help that was given to him.

"It's a start let's take it one step at a time we'll just have to be on our guard. Now come on let's get you back to Ixor before the king changes his mind." Ordmin said as they climbed the steps towards the knight's freedom.

Reclaiming his horse within the castle grounds Sir Endevoure said to Ordmin. "What have you done with the princess is she safe and is there a chance I could see her."

Ordmin could not answer straight away as he was struggling to mount his horse, once the squire had managed to hitch him in the air he slumped down onto his saddle with a thud and then he said. "She is safe her maids are under my strict instructions not to leave her side. No I'm sorry you can't see her It would complicate the situation, let's sort out this mess first then we will be able to help her."

The drawbridge again was lowered to let the two men ride towards Ixor's encampment. Standing there outside his canopy Ixor watched as the two riders were allowed to approach him. "It's good to see you both again but where's princess Collesta." Ixor said as he grabbed the reigns of Ordmin's horse.

"She is for the time being quite safe with her maids in her chambers." Ordmin said while sliding off his horse awkwardly with his legs almost giving way, straightening up he then said. "I've been sent by the king to give you a compromise which could settle this dispute once and for all."

"Come inside then I'm curious of what he has to say. Hello what's happened to you?" Ixor said seeing the bruised face of Sir Endevoure.

"These bruises are only borrowed give it time I'll have them repaid with interest you can be sure of it." Sir Endevoure said as he lowered his head while entering the marquee.

It was good to see his old teacher again but would he be able to trust him, Ixor thought as the old man began to explain how he was going to organize the tournament.

Chapter Twelve

The next day Ordmin with the king's personal helpers along with some of Ixor's soldiers began to organize the setting out of the tournament's site just outside the castle walls. The decision was made that each side's marquees would be positioned at either end of the jousting range. That afternoon all was ready with all competing knights along with their own personal squire's took their positions in their own marquee areas. On the side of the king you had five minor knights plus Sir Bellingham, Sir Blades and Sir Raymond the Blue, Green and Yellow knights, eight competitors in all. Whereas Ixor made his side up with the best horsemen he had along with himself and Sir Endevoure.

Early afternoon Ordmin and the king who was well protected with many of his personal bodyguards took to their seats in the stands which were positioned between the outside of the castle walls and along one side of the dueling arena.

A draw of who was to compete against who had been decided earlier that day. There were four jousting lanes so two contests would be fought at any one time. First to battle was Sir Blades and Sir Bellingham against two of Ixor's horsemen, the outcome was inevitable, both of Ixor's men hit the dust after receiving blows to their chests from their opponents well directed lances.

Next in line Sir Endevoure and Ixor against two minor knights, the result almost a repeat of the first battle only this time in reverse both of the king's men hit the dust after flying from their horses.

The third duel was two minor knights against two of Ixor's horsemen that ended in a draw with both sides losing one man in each bout.

It was now Sir Raymond with a minor knight to compete against two more of Ixor's horsemen, again a bad result for Ixor as both his men left their saddles from blows their shields failed to stop.

Watching the tournament the king stood up and cheered every time his side triumphed against his opponents. Seeing this Ixor turned to his men telling them that whatever the outcome on this day they would all still be his champions. "Do your best just try to stay in one piece," He said as he watched Sir Endevoure and his last horseman mount up to be ready for their joust. Down at the opposite end Sir Blades with a minor knight waited for the off. Both sides charged towards each other with lances poised for the strike. For the first time in this contest two true knights battled for supremacy.

Revenge was sweat for the Black knight when his lance made contact with the head of Sir Blades knocking him backwards from his horse with such force causing him to comatose upon the ground. At the same time Ixor's horseman defeated the minor knight. The king now did not look as happy as he did earlier with the odds now equal on both sides.

Two squires carried off Sir Blades on a stretcher. Ixor and Sir Endevoure prepared for the penultimate contest between Sir Raymond and the last of the minor knights. The two sides charged towards each other at such speed that the lances of Ixor and Sir Raymond brushed each other's shield whereas Sir Endevoure again dismounted his opponent.

Turning at each other's end the two knights charged again this time Ixor succeeded with his lance powering through shield and rider causing his opponents horse's front legs to buckle beneath its weight somersaulting the green knight through the air landing him on his back.

Now with only Sir Bellingham left Ixor decided to let Sir Endevoure have the chance of the last joust knowing the knights grievance was greater than his own. "Anyway If you lose I'll get my chance to have a go, whatever happens I'm sure one of us will topple him." Ixor said.

"Don't worry I'll make sure he tastes the dirt before this days over, It's something I've been looking forward to his days are numbered you can be sure of it." Sir Endevoure said as he prepared to ride towards his jousting lane.

After the knight left Ixor looked over towards the king to see him signal towards the castle battlements, "Now what's he up to I don't think he's going to obey by the rules we'll have to be on our guard." Ixor thought.

The middle barriers shook as the Black and Blue knights thundered towards each other both lances snapped from their direct hit upon each other's shield. Riding back to collect another lance both knights charged again, this time only the horses were still standing after the two riders simultaneously succeeded in knocking each other to the ground. Now with swords drawn the two started to battle on, the sword fight continued for ten minutes until the strength of Sir Endevoure conquered through to beat Sir Bellingham, the force of knocking him to the ground took his helmet off, and with the sword of Sir Endevoure aimed at his throat Sir Bellingham conceded defeat.

Now with the upper hand Sir Endevoure took the opportunity to say. "Do you swear allegiance to the true king, king Ixor Victinours or would you like to die now?"

Gasping for air Sir Bellingham answered. "I would prefer to live so I think I'd better swear allegiance to the new king."

Just as the Black knight began to help his opponent to his feet the cheers from Ixor's men were turned into shouts of horror there on the battlements between two of the kings henchmen was princess Collesta struggling with hysterical screams her two captors waited for the kings command to throw her from the battlements. This action of the king put the whole of Ixor's army on alert. Grabbing their weapons they rushed forward to protect their mentors.

At the same time the bodyguard of the king rushed forward to protect him by surrounding him from any harm. Ordmin who was sitting beside the king was pushed to one side, turning to the king he said. "Sire I made a promise to protect the princess now you have broken that trust. Why?"

"Stop whining you old fool, time I got rid of you." The king said as he ordered one of his men to attack Ordmin with his sword, which he did with a thrust into the side of the old man killing him immediately.

When this dirty deed was done the king averted his attentions to the battlements, with one quick wave to the two men holding the princess, they threw her from the battlements to a certain death.

Ixor with his army stood there powerless as they watched in horror, until a recognizable shrill sounded from out of the sky, it was a great bird carrying Sir Favour the white knight on its back swooping in with its talons the bird snatched the princess from her fall then carried her off towards the trees at the rear of Ixor's forces.

The knights had always respected Ordmin, killing him the king had gone too far they now all swore allegiance to

Ixor their true king, the king seeing this quickly retreated with his men back towards the castle with Ixor and his followers in pursuit.

The order was given for the archers of Ixor to fire a volley of arrows at the king before he reached the castle. Some of the arrows met their targets with devastating affect most of the kings bodyguard received an arrow, now with half of his protection gone an arrow managed to find its way through to hit the king in the arm. The drawbridge was lowered as the king with the rest of his men limped inside to the safety of the castle.

The next volley of arrows hit the drawbridge as it was raised. Archers on the battlements retaliated with their own arrows forcing Ixor with his riders to retreat to beyond their range.

Regrouping his men Ixor encircled the castle again with his archers and infantry while his knights, himself with his cavalry made camp to the rear of his forces to discuss their next move of attack.

With all the knights on his side Ixor left Sir Endevoure in command to restart the siege of the castle as he with

Sir Blades rode back towards the forest to find princess Collesta and Sir Favour his friend.

Riding together Ixor turned to Sir Blades and said. “I shall miss Ordmin he would have been a good adviser for my future as king he will be very hard to replace.”

Sir Blades said. “Yes we shall all miss him but I think you will find you will now have all the knight’s to support you so don’t worry.”

With these comforting words the darkness of the night was drawing in they both realized they would have to find the young knight and her highness quickly.

Chapter Thirteen

It took only five minutes through the forest when they both noticed a bright light ahead through the trees. It was a fire Sir Favour had lit to keep himself with the princess warm. As the two riders appeared from out of the trees they could see Sir Favour with sword in his hand having to ward off a pack of wolves, slicing and cutting he had slain four of the curs, with about ten more to deal with his strength now looked about spent. Princess Collesta was sitting close to the fire shaking with fear and holding a large thick branch ready to ward off the wolves.

"Hold on sir knight we are coming we'll kill the bastards." Sir Blades shouted as he sliced through one of the wolves with his sword while leaning to one side from his saddle. Ixor too annihilated one of the animals before sliding from his horse to join his friend. Now with three swords whistling in the air the wolves decided enough is enough except for the largest and blackest of beasts who had managed to pass through the cordon of knights to within the reach of her highness, panicking she hit it with the branch then lost her grip, with the branch out of the way the wolf began to bite with its teeth upon her boot. Without hesitation Ixor turned then threw himself upon the wolves back with his sword in both hands he thrust it straight down through between the shoulder blades of the wolf killing it instantly.

Leaving the wolf for dead Ixor lifted the princess to her feet, cuddling her in his arms he said. "Are you hurt in any way?"

She replied." Not at all only a little shaken I thought I was about to be eaten by that beast thanks to you and Sir Favour I'll survive, I knew you would find a way of saving me."

Sir Blades dismounted from his horse then led it over to where Ixor's horse stood then tied them both to a tree then approached Sir Favour who stood there drained from exhaustion and said. "Was that bird you were on a vulcrom I thought I killed the last one with my lance?"

Taking his helmet off from his head the knackered knight replied. "It was and you did kill its mother but this one was from one of her eggs. On the night after you killed her I climbed the cliff again and rescued the two remaining eggs left in the nest, that same night I took the eggs to a relative nearby who with my help over the next two years mothered the two chicks, so now they think they are my children and now will do anything for me."

With his mouth wide open Sir Blades could hardly believe at what he had just heard. "So there are two of them flying around, how is it you can contact them when you need them." He said disbelieving.

Taking a small whistle from his tunic Sir Favour said. "With this they come whenever I blow upon it without fail. Lately only one has been turning up I do believe the other one has laid some eggs so soon I shall become a grandfather."

Holding princess Collesta by the hand Ixor said to Sir Favour. "How did you know the princess was in trouble you were supposed to be at the garrison, tell us we are dying to know?"

Sir Favour answered. "Lord Darnley became worried for you so he decided to look into the book of knowledge where he saw the princess was in trouble he then asked me if I knew of a way of saving her, of course I knew exactly what I could do so I whistled for the vulcrom the rest you know."

Everything now started to make sense for Ixor he knew he would always be in Sir Favours debt, he then said. "We shall make camp here for the night. Sir Blades will take the first watch in case the wolves come back."

The princess was made comfortable for the night on a bed of soft heather, now with the fire stoked up everyone managed to get some sleep even between shifts of watch which they all took in turn.

Next morning as soon as the light appeared Ixor told Sir Blades to let Sir Favour have his horse so he could take the princess back to the garrison where she would be safe. Before she left Ixor promised he would return to the princess as soon as he had conquered the king and his followers. Saying their goodbyes they reluctantly parted as Ixor with Sir Blades rode off on the other horse in the opposite direction towards the siege of the castle.

Chapter Fourteen

The two knights on their charger arrived back at the edge of the forest only to find that Sir Endevoure had ordered the men to chop many of the trees down and were now busy building two large assault towers. Also ropes in large quantity from bark fibre and creepers were being weaved with most of the dead wood used for large fire pyres, the heat was intense from these fires as he passed by them. Ixor noticed several farrier's busy at work on their anvils making large hook eyes. Ixor called to one of the horse shoe makers. "Why are you all making these contraptions I would have thought you would have been making weapons for the battle?"

Noticing it was the war lord talking to him the iron maker bowed then said. "Sir we have no idea of what they are for only that Sir Endevoure instructed us to make them as soon as possible."

Ixor said. “Very well carry on.” Then rode on towards the knight’s standard which was flapping in the wind outside a large marquee.

Arriving back at the main marquee Ixor and Sir Blades dismounted in front of Sir Endevoure who stood there waiting with all the other knights for a meeting to decide the next plan of action.

“Did you find the princess and was she ok?” said Sir Endevoure as he with all the other knight’s led Ixor to seats inside the marquee where food and drink was about to be served up from all of their squire’s.

Sitting down to rest was lovely for Ixor especially after the action he had been involved in the last few days. “Yes she is well I have sent her back with Sir Favour to the garrison. I see you have all been busy, that’s a good idea building those towers but what are those large iron rings for I noticed being made by the farrier’s?”

“Ah you will see tomorrow its one of Sir Bellingham’s brain child ideas he has been quite helpful while you’ve been away.” Sir Endevoure said as he sat down next to Ixor before asking a squire to serve up the food and wine.

Next day the archers were positioned strategically in front of the castle behind their shields they set up a barrage of arrows aimed at the battlements, while the inhabitants of the castle kept their heads down two groups of eight men from Ixor's army carrying the four iron rings rushed forward to each of the two turrets positioned at either end of the castle, under the safety of the base of the walls they began with large anvil hammers to smash in two rings on each turret.

Stones rocks and other items were being thrown from the turrets but to no avail the ring invaders were too close to the base of the walls any missile would have landed too far out to make any impact.

With all the rings firmly in place Ixor's men managed to safely escape back to their own lines to the cheers of their own army they were greeted with pats on their backs.

Satisfied his men had succeeded Sir Endevoure turned to Ixor and the other knights and said. "Tonight in the dark I'll send some more men along with the four long ropes to thread the ends through the rings then they can bring the ropes back and attach them to the sides of the nearly finished towers."

Next morning after the nights work had been successfully completed Sir Bellingham told the others the towers would be ready in another two days. “Let’s hope the weather changes to rain it would be to our advantage we don’t want the enemy using fire arrows against us when we tow the towers into position.” Sir Bellingham said.

“Good idea it’s decided then we wait for rain on the day we attack in force, make sure everyone stays on high alert for the next few days so with every ones approval I suggest we keep the men busy at mock fighting.” Sir Endevoure said.

A week passed and in that time twice the drawbridge lowered with riders appearing to attack in force against Ixor’s army each time they were forced back into the castle under a volley of arrows.

The day came when the heavens opened the rain dropped like a waterfall. Ixor said to his knight’s. “Get the men ready to bring the towers forward today is the day we attack.”

The other end of the ropes were tethered to four groups of six heavy set horses, under the lash these horses began to pull in the opposite direction from the rings these heavy manned towers towards the turrets of the castle.

These towers were built higher than the turrets, in position the castles archers found it awkward to aim their arrows upward against the driving rain whereas Ixor's archers had the advantage from the top of the towers of firing downward and across the battlements. After killing many of the kings men from the cross fire of arrows the infantry behind the archers from within the towers waited for their command to strike.

A large ramp from each tower was lowered onto the battlements allowing the infantry to charge and fight their way through the remaining enemy.

With the drawbridge being lowered defeat was quick with the rest of the castles inhabitants surrendering under a white flag to Ixor's cavalry of knights carrying their lances when they charged in to the grounds.

It was obvious to Ixor and his knights the people of the castle were hungry they looked tired from exhaustion with many who found it hard to stand.

Dismounting from their horses Ixor with his knights walked across the court yard to the main building, on entering through the door at the top of the steps they met no resistance from within all squires and servants bowed their heads as Ixor passed them.

On entering the main hall the king was nowhere to be seen. Grabbing hold of a servant Sir Endevoure asked "where is the king? Take us to him now."

The servant who was trembling said. "Sir he is ill in his bed chamber he's been there since he was shot in the arm, if you follow me I'll show you where he is."

Knocking on the king's door a maid appeared then bowed as soon as she saw it was Ixor letting him in with his knights following behind they found a servant tending to the king who was dying in his bed. The servant turned to Ixor and said. "Sir the king would like to talk to you and Sir Endevoure alone."

As the other knights left the room the king beckoned the two knights to come closer to his bed side, whispering to them in a frail condition he said. "I never wanted it to come to this but you pushed me into a situation I could not escape from only now I would like you Sir Endevoure to be a witness to my last will and testament." He then handed a parchment to the knight and asked him to read it out aloud in front of Ixor.

Opening the parchment the knight began to read. "I king Hobart Victinours hereby bequest the throne its castle of Tonest with all the lands and buildings surrounding it to my nephew Ixor Victinours in the hope he will become a true and just king.

The knight had just finished reading it when the kings breathing started to falter as he held his quill in his hand ready to sign. "Bring it to me let me sign." The king said. Signing the parchment with his last breath his hand slid to his side as he died.

Next day the bodies of the dead were taken outside the castle grounds for burial the king's funeral was arranged to take place on a hill to the rear of the castle.

After his uncle's funeral Ixor was pronounced the new king in front of all his knights with Sir Endevoure placing the crown upon his head he then said the words. "I being a true knight of the castle Tonest crown Ixor Victinours Knight of the Dragon Red to be our king."

As soon as he was crowned a big cheer with the words long live the king sounded from in and around the castle grounds.

Two days later after all the clearing up from the battle King Ixor with Sir Endevoure left the other knights to take charge of the castle while they with half the army returned to the garrison.

On their return they were cheered again from the settlement. Outside the manor house Lord Darnley his daughter lady Silvianda and princess Collesta were waiting for their love ones.

Before dismounting from his horse Ixor said. "Where is my friend Sir Favour is he not here?"

Lord Darnley laughing said. "He was called away to the nest to see the birth of his grandchildren."

As they dismounted they all started laughing. "So he is going to be a granddad then I hope he will be very happy." Ixor replied.

Two weeks later back at the castle everyone attended the marriage of King Ixor and his bride Princess Collester. Her father King Plestoe managed to travel from his lands to attend.

After the marriage they walked under an arch of swords from the knights holding them, they were all there Sir Endevoure, Sir Bellingham, Sir Raymond, Sir Blades, and of course, Sir Favour who was the best man.

From the masses of people watching a shout was heard LONG LIVE KING IXOR KNIGHT OF THE DRAGON RED.

Lightning Source UK Ltd.
Milton Keynes UK
07 February 2011

166920UK00001BB/3/P